Hello, Family Members,

Learning to read is one of the most important accomplishments of early childhood. *Hello Readers* are designed to help children become skilled readers who like to read. Beginning readers learn to read by remembering frequently used words like "the," "is," and "and"; by using phonics skills to decode new words; and by interpreting picture and text clues. These books provide both the stories children enjoy and the structure they need to read fluently and independently. Here are suggestions for helping your child *before*, *during*, and *after* reading:

Before

- Look at the cover and pictures and have your child predict what the story is about.
- Read the story to your child.
- Encourage your child to chime in with familiar words and phrases.
- Echo read with your child by reading a line first and having your child read it after you do.

During

- Have your child think about a word he or she does not recognize right away. Provide hints such as "Let's see if we know the sounds" and "Have we read other words like this one?"
- Encourage your child to use phonics skills to sound out new words.
- Provide the word for your child when more assistance is needed so that he or she does not struggle and the experience of reading with you is a positive one.
- Encourage your child to have fun by reading with a lot of expression . . . like an actor!

After

- Have your child keep lists of interesting and favorite words.
- Encourage your child to read the books over and over again. Have him or her read to brothers, sisters, grandparents, and even teddy bears. Repeated readings develop confidence in young readers.
- Talk about the stories. Ask and answer questions. Share ideas about the funniest and most interesting characters and events in the stories.

I do hope that you and your child enjoy this book.

—Francie Alexander
Reading Specialist,
Scholastic's Instructional Publishing Group

If you have questions or comments about how children learn to read, please contact Francie Alexander at FrancieAl@aol.com

To tropical Jac
— L.J.H.

Text copyright © 1998 by Lorraine Jean Hopping.
Illustrations copyright © 1998 by Jody Wheeler.
All rights reserved. Published by Scholastic Inc.
HELLO READER! and CARTWHEEL BOOKS and associated logos
are trademarks and/or registered trademarks of Scholastic Inc.

Library of Congress Cataloging-in-Publication Data
Hopping, Lorraine Jean.
    Wild weather: Blizzards!/by Lorraine Jean Hopping; illustrated by Jody Wheeler.
        p.   cm.—(Hello reader! Level 4)
    "Cartwheel Books."
    Summary: Describes the incredible power of blizzards, from the blizzards of 1888 to blizzards in 1997; tells what makes a blizzard and how scientists try to forecast them.
    ISBN 0-590-39730-3
    1. Blizzards—United States—Juvenile literature.
[1. Blizzards.]   I. Wheeler, Jody, ill.   II. Title.   III. Series.
QC926.43.U6H66   1998
551.55'5—dc21   97-28520
                                                                          CIP
                                                                          AC

10 9 8 7 6 5 4 3 2 1   8 9/9 0/0 01 02

Printed in the U.S.A.   24

First printing, January 1998

⚡ WILD WEATHER ⚡

Blizzards!

by Lorraine Jean Hopping
Illustrated by Jody Wheeler

Hello Reader! Science — Level 4

SCHOLASTIC INC. Cartwheel B·O·O·K·S ®

New York   Toronto   London   Auckland   Sydney

Chapter 1

The Killer Blizzards of '88

The winters of 1886 and 1887
were scary.
In the northern Plains,
cattle froze to death.
Farmers nearly starved.
But the next winter, the winter
of 1888, was sheer terror.
It began with mild, springlike
weather.
On January 12, children
played outside without coats!

Within hours, the mild weather took a shocking turn.
School children in the Dakotas (now North and South Dakota) spotted the storm during recess. It raced toward them across the big prairie sky.
One witness said the clouds were like "big bales of cotton, each one bound tightly."

These "cotton bales" soon
covered the prairie like a dark,
fluffy blanket.
But this "blanket" did not
bring comfort and warmth.
It brought snow, biting wind,
and freezing cold.
A killer blizzard had hit!

The storm marched into
Nebraska.
Teacher Minnie Freeman, age
eighteen, acted fast.
She herded her class into the
schoolhouse.
But the building was made of
sod, not brick.
The howling wind began to rip it
apart.

Minnie tied all thirteen children together with twine.
Then she led the class toward a sturdy, wooden shack.
The strong wind made walking almost impossible.
The blowing snow blocked everything from sight.
But the children made it to the shack.
Minnie was a hero!

Another teacher named Grace McCoy saved her class, too.
She did it by burning every chair, every table, and every stick of wood.
Then, with no fuel left, the temperature in the school dipped below freezing.

"After midnight, it seemed to me we would all die," Grace said.
But a few hours later, an eerie quiet fell.
The storm had ended.
The children went home.

Not everyone survived the blizzard of 1888.
More than five hundred people died.
Then, just two months later, the same sad story began again.

March 10, 1888, was the
warmest day of the year in New
York City.
"More fair weather tomorrow,"
said one forecast.
"A little colder with a chance of
light snow," said another.
Both forecasts were wrong.

South of New York, in Delaware,
temperatures dropped.
Rain turned into a wall of snow.
The wind reached hurricane
speed — 75 miles per hour.
The anchor cables of ships
snapped like worn guitar strings.
Two hundred ships sank.

The blizzard raced up the east coast at 80 miles per hour. But no one could warn the people in its path. Telegraph and telephone lines were down. And carrier pigeons couldn't carry messages in the storm.

That night, the blizzard slammed into New York City. The wind blew streetcars off their tracks! "Snow fell like buckets of flour thrown from the rooftops," said Arthur Bier, who was in New York City during the storm. Albany, New York, had almost four feet of snow in one day! Four hundred people died in all.

Both blizzards of 1888 are among
the worst in history.

Chapter 2

Snowing, Blowing, and Cold

A blizzard is not just a bad snowstorm.

It's also a bad windstorm.

Every blizzard has winds that blow 35 miles per hour or more.

That's strong enough to make even big trees shake!

A severe blizzard is one that has 45-mile-per-hour winds.

Just staying on your feet is a major battle!

Blizzard winds blow tons of snow
into the air.
The result is a whiteout.
The sky, the ground—
everything—looks white.
During a whiteout, people can't
even see objects a few feet away.
Some people have frozen to
death just steps from their door!

To be a blizzard, a storm needs more than just wind and snow. It also needs Arctic cold. Every blizzard feels like 20 degrees* below zero or colder. Windchill is a measurement of how cold the air feels.

Here's how windchill works: The thermometer may read 10 degrees. That's cold. But the air *feels* even colder when the wind is blowing. That's why, on wintry days, people should stay out of the wind.

A wind blowing 20 miles per hour makes 10 degrees feel like 24 degrees below zero (see chart). Brrr!

*Temperatures are in Fahrenheit.

WINDCHILL FORMULA

Wind Speed	Temperature	Windchill Factor
When the wind blows...	and the thermometer reads...	then the temperature feels like...
10 mph	10° F	−9° F
20 mph	10° F	−24° F
30 mph	10° F	−33° F

WINDCHILL EFFECTS

Windchill Factor (how cold it feels)	Effects
0 to 15	Very cold
−15 to 0	Bitter cold
−30 to −15	Bare skin starts to freeze
below −30	Bare skin freezes in seconds

A low windchill can freeze skin
in minutes and turn it pale.
Dead, frozen skin is called
frostbite.
The fingers, toes, ears, and nose
usually freeze first.
But any bare skin is in danger of
frostbite during a blizzard.

In 1982, a 17-year-old rock
climber named Hugh Herr tried
to fight off frostbite.
A storm trapped him and a
friend on Mount Washington,
New Hampshire.
The mountain holds the record
for the fastest wind in the
United States: 231 miles
per hour!

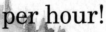

Walking against the strong wind, Hugh and his friend grew tired. They knew that moving makes the blood flow and the body stay warm.

But Hugh could not move another step.

His legs began to turn numb.

Three days later, rescuers found the climbers.

Hugh's friend recovered.

He had never stopped moving.

But Hugh lost both lower legs to frostbite.

Later, he learned to climb again using special artificial legs.

In time, he scaled tougher mountains than before the accident!

Seven out of ten blizzard victims
die in cars stuck in the snow.
The cause is hypothermia, or
low body temperature.
Normal bodies are 98.6 degrees.
At just a few degrees cooler, the
body starts to fail.
The heart and lungs slow down.
The brain gets confused.
At 55 degrees, the victim may
die.

In 1997, Karen Nelson of North
Dakota drove off-course in a
whiteout.
Her truck got stuck in the snow.
The gas gauge dipped to low and
then empty.
After forty chilling hours,
rescuers found Karen.
Her body was blue with
hypothermia.

But doctors raised her body
temperature just in time.

Chapter 3

Superstorm

Blizzards are common in Canada and north central United States. They often visit northern Europe and Russia.

And they are right at home on mountains and in polar regions. But people in warm climates aren't totally safe.

In 1993, a blizzard known as "Superstorm" stretched from Vermont to Florida. Sixty thousand flashes of lightning hit the ground! Tornadoes spun out of the clouds! Few blizzards have lightning and tornadoes.

Superstorm 1993

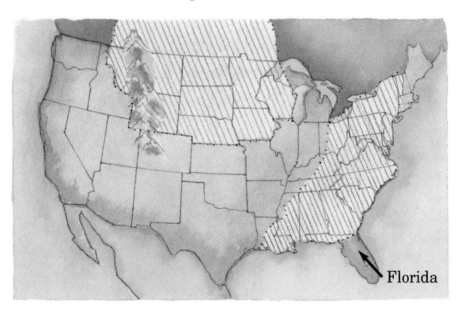

Florida

░ Frequent blizzards   ░ Superstorm

About 270 people died in
Superstorm.
Many deaths were in southern
states such as Florida.
There, people were less prepared
to cope with a blizzard.

Why do killer blizzards form?
In 1888, people had no idea.
Minnie and her class didn't
know what hit them.
How could the temperature drop
50 degrees in a few hours?
Why did the wind grow so fierce?
Weather scientists have
found some of the answers.

In winter, Arctic air masses
sweep into the United States
from Canada.
They can travel as fast as a
speeding car.
At the same time, warm air
masses enter the United States
from the south.
They are bursting with moisture.

Arctic,
dry air

What happens when the two air masses crash?

Instant winter storm: cold, wind, and snow.

The temperature drops as the Arctic air pushes the warm air out of the way.

very warm, moist air

Cold and warm air swirl around
each other.
The lighter warm air may roll
over the heavy cold air.
The cold air may push the warm
air from below.
We feel this moving, shoving,
swirling air as wind.
As the wet, warm air cools off,
the clouds shrink.

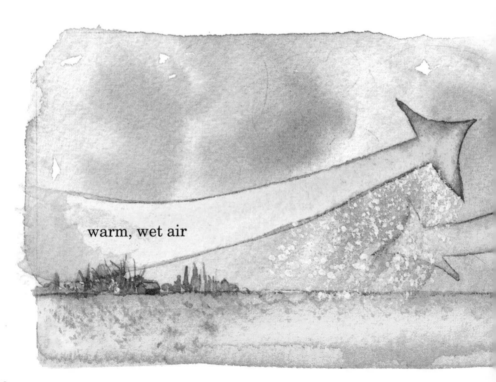

warm, wet air

The process is similar to
squeezing a wet sponge.
Shrunken clouds can't hold as
much moisture.
So snowflakes or ice crystals
fall out of them.
After a blizzard, the wind stops.
The temperature may rise.
Only the snow remains to cause
more life-threatening problems.

cool, dry air

Chapter 4

Mountains of Snow

Storms pick up moisture as they
pass over lakes.
Then they dump the moisture on
areas near the lakes.
Buffalo, New York, is one of
these "lake effect" cities.
In a 1977 blizzard, snow drifted
30 feet high there.
That's enough to bury trucks
and entire houses!

The drifts were so high that deer
escaped from the zoo.
They simply walked over the
snow-covered fence!
Buffalo residents shoveled up to
four tons of snow per driveway.

Buffalo, NY

In January 1996, snow on New York City streets was piled high.
Cars were buried.
There was no place left to put the snow!
For days, dump trucks hauled snow out of the city.

Giant snowdrifts don't just cause problems in cities.
A farmer named Brad Olson almost got clobbered by one.
A 1997 blizzard in Minnesota dumped 20 inches of heavy snow on his barn.
Brad ran out of the barn seconds before the roof fell.

If blizzard snow melts, floods
may take more lives or ruin
more property.
Even if the snow doesn't melt, it
creates a hazard on mountains.
There, blizzards pile snow at
steep angles.
Picture a pile of flour on a
cookie sheet.
Lift one end of the sheet higher,
bit by bit.

At some point, the whole pile
slides down—fast!

Lots of snow sliding or falling
down a slope is an avalanche.
The snow can travel faster than
a speeding train!
Skiers, climbers, and others in
the area can get buried.

Chapter 5

The Next Big Blizzard

How can we know for sure when
the next blizzard will hit?
Scientist John Cortinas asks
that question every day.
But he can't always answer it.
Not even the biggest computer
in the world can be one hundred
percent sure of the weather.

John works at the National
Severe Storms Laboratory in
Oklahoma.
He studies past storms for clues
that signal a storm is forming or
changing.

The clues might be a certain mix
of temperature, wind speed, air
pressure, and humidity (wetness).

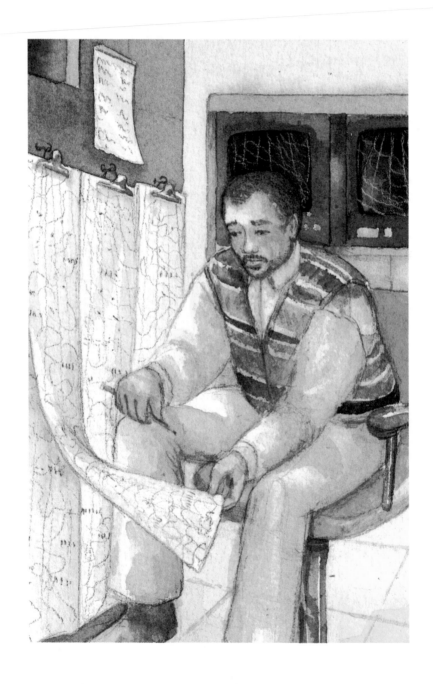

Scientists at the National Weather Service look for similar clues in current weather. They study a computer weather map like the one at right. Then they enter all the data into a supercomputer. An hour or so later, the computer makes a forecast called a model.

The model shows how weather is likely to change over time. For example, it might predict temperatures twelve hours into the future. Models aren't always right. In fact, models from two different computers can disagree.

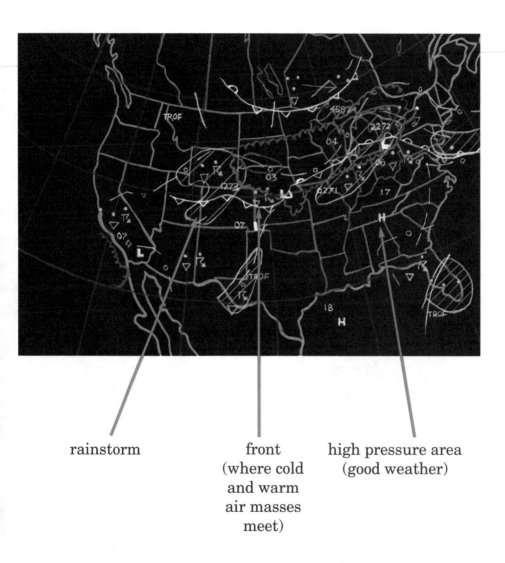

rainstorm   front
(where cold
and warm
air masses
meet)

high pressure area
(good weather)

In January 1996, one computer model showed heavy snow heading for the northeast. Another called for light rain. It predicted the storm would stay at sea. Weather forecasters believed the model for heavy snow.

They put out a winter storm
warning.
And they were right.

How did the scientists know?
"The forecaster has to look at all
the data," John says, "not just the
computer model."

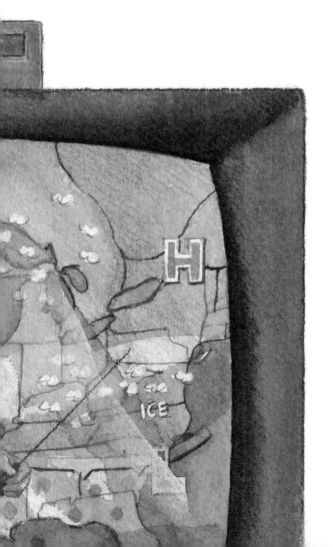

"All the data" includes models, radar images, and weather readings from around the world. John's research on past storms helps forecasters make sense of all this data on current storms.

Does a certain radar pattern mean a storm is getting worse? How can we tell if a storm will suddenly change course? What happens when a storm moves from sea to land?

The more answers that scientists find, the more certain forecasters can be. They can confidently say that a killer blizzard is — or isn't — on the way.

Blizzard Tips

- In cold weather, always wear a bright coat, three layers of clothes, mittens, boots, and a hat. Never go off alone.
- A blizzard watch means a storm may form.
A blizzard warning means a storm is on the way.
In either case, stay inside!
- If you are stuck outside, stay in your car or find shelter.
Put a bright object where rescuers might see it.
Keep moving! Clap your hands.
Jump up and down.
And don't fall asleep!